F R A S E R

Maggie

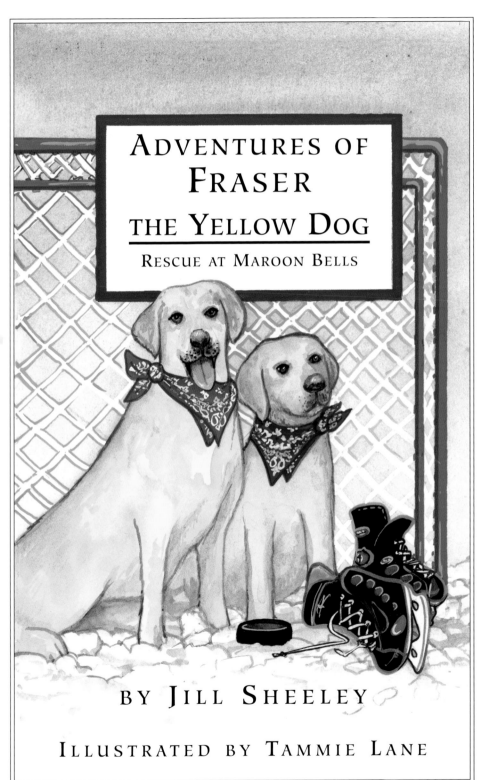

ADVENTURES OF FRASER
THE YELLOW DOG
RESCUE AT MAROON BELLS

BY JILL SHEELEY

ILLUSTRATED BY TAMMIE LANE

COURTNEY PRESS

First edition published in 2007 by Courtney Press, Aspen, Colorado
Copyright © 2007 by Jill Sheeley

A very special thanks to Rob Seideman, Tammie Lane, Kathy Reppa, Hensley Peterson, Scott Arthur, Brent Perusse, Martha Moran, students at Aspen Elementary School, my family and all my many friends who gave me advice and support.

This is a fictional story. The girls, Fraser and Maggie go snowmobiling and ice-skating unsupervised for the sake of adventure in this story. In real life, the author recommends snowmobiling and skating with a knowledgeable adult. It is advised to keep pets on a leash when on strong, tested ice. The dogs are off-leash in this story for the sake of conflict and resolution.

For more information about ordering this book, write: Jill Sheeley • P.O. Box 845 • Aspen, CO 81612. Check out our website: www.jillsheeleybooks.com

Printed in Korea
ISBN 978-0-9795592-0-4

Mail us your rescue stories to: Jill Sheeley • P.O. Box 845 • Aspen, CO 81612.

Visit us on the web at www.jillsheeleybooks.com

I'd like to dedicate this book to the thousands of Fraser fans around the world. I keep writing because of you. To Don, Courtney and my wonderful parents who give me inspiration and unending support.

To Chris Klug, and Gretchen Bleiler — two Olympic Snowboard Champions from Aspen who inspire us all.

Partial Proceeds from this book will benefit the Aspen Animal Shelter.

Special thanks to Marie at the Scandinavian Design shop in Aspen for allowing Tammie to paint the gorgeous Scandinavian sweaters sold at her shop. For more information, contact Marie at www.aspenscandes.com; 675 E. Cooper Ave., Aspen CO 81611; 970-925-7299.

Thanks to Paradise Bakery in Aspen for being such generous sponsors! Be sure to check out their wonderful home-baked cookies, muffins and Italian-style ice creams. Visit them on the corner of Galena Street and Cooper Avenue.

Thanks to ESPN for allowing us to use the Winter X Games in this book.

Did you hear the news?" asked Courtney as she and her friends marched through the Winter X Games entrance. "The lake at Maroon Bells is frozen. We can skate on it!"

"That hasn't happened in 50 years," said Katy.

"It's a dream come true," said Taylor. "Maroon Bells is the most magical place in the world."

"We better get there before everyone else finds out," said Katy.

"Fraser and Maggie can come, too!" said Courtney.

"How are we going to get there?" asked Katy. "The road to Maroon Bells isn't plowed 'til spring."

"I bet my dad will loan us his snowmobiles," said Courtney.

"Perfect," said Taylor. "Let's meet at T Lazy 7 Ranch tomorrow morning."

"Sounds like a plan," said Courtney. Just then, a local snowboarder soared high over their heads. The girls screamed and whistled.

"Don't forget the chocolate chip cookies, Courtney," said Katy.

The llamas at T Lazy 7 Ranch were just waking up when the girls arrived.

"Did you guys bring ice awls and shovels?" asked Courtney. "If not, I have extras, plus I brought our radio phone, first aid gear and my dad's rescue throw bag."

"I was so excited this morning I almost forgot my hockey skates," laughed Taylor.

"Maggie," said Courtney, "you're too young to run all the way, so you can ride on the snowmobile with me."

"Ready Fraser?" asked Courtney.

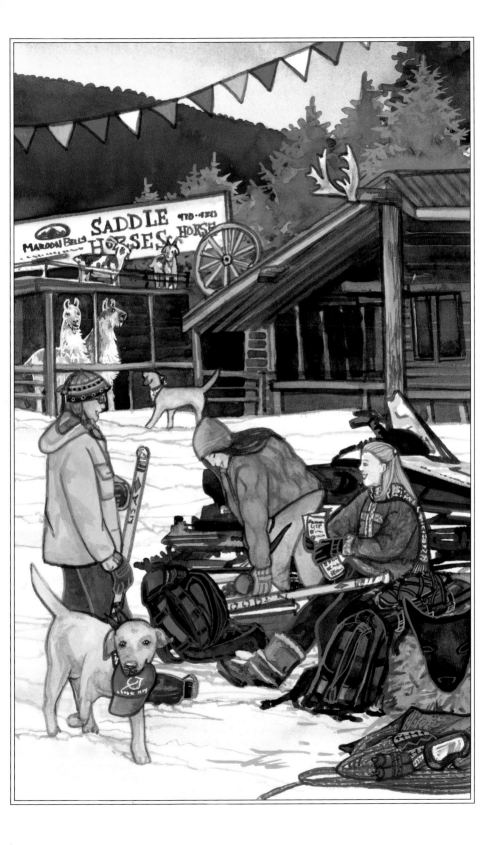

The day was cloudless and cold. The girls hooted and hollered as they rode over the rippled road leading up to the Maroon Bells.

"Hang on, Maggie," said Katy.

"Let's stop up ahead," Courtney yelled over the roar of the snowmobile. "We can have a quick snack."

"Sounds good to me," screamed back Taylor, "I'm always hungry."

"Wow," said Katy, "these cookies are yummy. What's different about them?"

"I added peanut butter this time," said Courtney. "What do you think?"

"I say let's save our fruit for later," laughed Taylor.

"Did you know," asked Courtney, "that in 2001 a hiker discovered the tracks of prehistoric creatures called Diadectes at the Maroon Bells?"

"We just studied them in our science class," said Katy. "They have the head of a turtle and the body of a lizard."

"Cool," said Taylor, "no one's been here. There are no human tracks."

"Now we know how those creatures felt millions of years ago here at the Bells," said Katy.

"I'd better test the ice so we can skate," said Courtney.

"What's that?" asked Katy, looking at the stick in Courtney's hand.

"It's an *unaak*. My dad and I made it together. It's an ice probe and a self-rescue tool all in one. All I have to do is thrust the spike into the ice. If it feels mushy, the ice isn't good. If it bounces back, we're OK. I'll probe every few steps just to make sure."

"We're good to go," said Courtney.

"This is amazing," said Taylor. "Do you realize where we are?"

The girls looked up at the majesty of the famous Maroon Bells.

"It feels special," said Courtney.

The girls were quiet for a moment until Fraser barked.

"Let's skate," said Katy.

"Let's play Shinney," said Courtney.

"What's that?" asked Taylor.

"It's a pond hockey game my dad used to play," said Courtney.

"We could take turns being goalie. After each score, we could switch positions. That way we can practice passing," said Katy.

"Just remember your ice awls," said Courtney.

"Let's play," said Taylor.

"Hey, where's Maggie going with our puck?" asked Katy.

Maggie pranced off proudly with the puck in her mouth.

"Come back, Maggie," yelled Taylor.

But when Maggie didn't come back with the puck, Courtney offered to get it.

She skated off after Maggie.

"Be careful, Courtney," cried Katy, "the ice may be thin over there."

But Courtney did not hear her.

"Drop it, Maggie," pleaded Courtney. "Drop it!"

Maggie ran around in circles, teasing Courtney.

All of a sudden, Courtney heard the ice around her crackle and splinter.

She knew she was in trouble.

Courtney fell quickly through the ice into the freezing lake water below. Wicked cold crept into her lower body. It took a moment, but then her instincts kicked in. She knew her ice awls were her only hope, and she grabbed them in both hands to stop her from falling further. Would they hold?

Courtney clung to the ice awls, paralyzed with fear.

"What should we do?" asked Katy.

Fraser was the first to respond. He pulled the rescue throw bag out of Courtney's backpack.

"Great idea," said Taylor.

Taylor skated over to Courtney. "Don't go any further," yelled Katy. "You'll fall in, too. Remember what we learned in our survival course? Stay calm, act quickly and call 911."

"Hang in there, Courtney," cried Taylor, "we're going to throw you the rope."

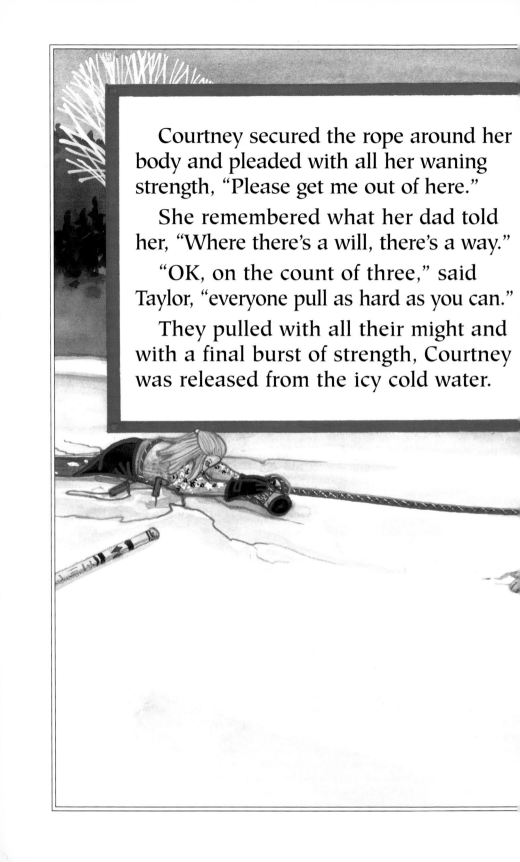

Courtney secured the rope around her body and pleaded with all her waning strength, "Please get me out of here."

She remembered what her dad told her, "Where there's a will, there's a way."

"OK, on the count of three," said Taylor, "everyone pull as hard as you can."

They pulled with all their might and with a final burst of strength, Courtney was released from the icy cold water.

Fraser and Maggie were keeping Courtney warm.

"Oh, Courtney," said Katy, "we're so glad you're OK. We were so scared."

"It's a good thing we brought extra clothes," said Taylor. "Drink some hot tea, Courtney, it will warm you up."

"Thanks everyone for saving me," said Courtney.

"Fraser got us moving to action," said Katy. "He never panics. He always knows just what to do."

Suddenly, everyone heard the rumbling of a snow cat in the distance.

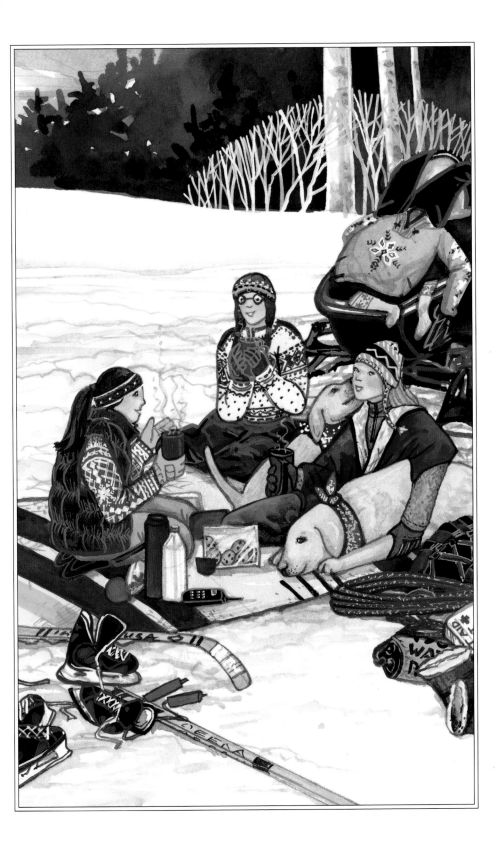

"Are you all right?" asked Mountain Rescue Rick. "We came as soon as we received your 911 call."

"Yes, thanks to Fraser and Maggie. They saved my life," said Courtney.

"And it looks like you did the right thing, too," said Ranger Jenny as she spotted Courtney's ice awls and heard the harrowing story. "How about a ride in our heated snow cat back to town for hot chocolate at Paradise Bakery?"

"Sounds good to me," said Courtney. "Can Fraser and Maggie come too?"

By the time they reached Paradise Bakery, the girls were warm and happy, singing songs and discussing the day.

Courtney held Fraser and Maggie close to her and exclaimed, "I can only wonder what our next adventure will be!"

☑ Never skate alone

☑ Never assume the ice is strong enough to hold you. Test the ice many times. It should be at least 5-6 inches thick

☑ Be prepared: carry ice awls, a probe pole (or unaak), extra clothing, a radio phone, first aid gear, rescue rope and other necessary items

☑ If you do fall through the ice, extend your hands and arms on to the unbroken surface and start kicking. As you come out of the water, don't stand up — lie on the ice and roll away

☑ When snowmobiling, never travel alone

☑ Tell someone your destination, route, and when you plan to return

☑ Be familiar with your snowmobile — carry extra spark plugs, tool kits and a towrope

☑ Carry a survival kit with map, compass, flashlight, extra food and clothing, first aid kit and other necessary items

☑ In case of emergencies, call 911 (do not rely on cell phones)

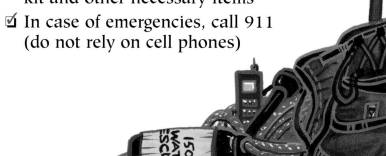